P9-AFE-543

One, two, three,
and down the
rabbit track with me.
Into a world of
well-heard words
That came from
my head like
a flock of birds.

With the most
curious habits
of always
turning into
stories of rabbits
One, two, three,
this book leads into
a green countree.

The GOLDEN BUNNY

AND 17 OTHER STORIES AND POEMS

by Margaret Wise Brown
pictures by Leonard Weisgard

A GOLDEN BOOK · NEW YORK
Western Publishing Company, Inc.
Racine, Wisconsin 53404

Copyright © 1953 by Western Publishing Company, Inc.
Copyright renewed 1981. All rights reserved. Printed in the U.S.A.
No part of this book may be reproduced or copied in any
form without written permission from the publisher.
GOLDEN®, GOLDEN & DESIGN®, and A GOLDEN BOOK® are
trademarks of Western Publishing Company, Inc.
ISBN 0-307-10416-8 / ISBN 0-307-60346-6 (lib. bdg.)
B C D E F G H I J

THE GOLDEN BUNNY

O best loved Bunny in all the world, this is the story of you.

Far off in a far country in a green green wood greener than most woods in this world, a Bunny opened his eyes.

He saw the winds blowing the ferns far above him and he never had heard of a tree.

Little shiny bugs crawled past him slower than he was.

And big black violets stared him right in the face with yellow violet eyes.

Star flowers bloomed over his head, and wild parsley and thyme, in this world of once upon a time when one bird sang for him alone.

And he went on and on in this wonderful world he had never seen before. Past a big gray stone to a running stream clear and cold to dip his nose in.

What a wonderful world, and the bird still sang.

And the ferns smelled warm at noon.

And he dozed there under a wild geranium that looked like a small wild rose. His little pink ears lay flat on his head, and his whiskers twitched as the bees flew by, and the first butterfly flew out of June and into July, in those northern woods so long ago. The Bunny fell asleep. And the shadows grew long, and the Bunny dreamed that the sun would never go down.

Then all at once he woke up!

He was alone!

Who was he?

What was he?

O bigger than a bug and smaller than a fern, you are lost!

O best loved Bunny in all the world. Lost in the cool green woods, and the sun will soon go down.

When the Bunny knew this, he jumped inside. Suddenly the world seemed very big and he seemed very little in it.

The Bunny ran into a green grass field.

But the sky was too big there.

He put his paws in the crystal stream.

But the water was too cold there.

He even jumped into the air.

But there was no ground there.

So he ran away.

And then he came back again.

And then he sat there.

He was lost.

He looked high above him, way up the long green stems.

What should he do now?

He twitched his nose.
He dangled his paws.
He flopped his ears.
He leaped in the air.

And then he thumped his hind legs bang on the ground. Thump — Bang! the sound echoed through the woods.

And soon, O best loved Bunny in all the world, his big warm mother came running to the side of her lost little Bunny and he wasn't lost anymore.

She took him home to his hollow tree and there she warmed him, the best loved Bunny in all the world. Warm and safe and warm.

And above in the night the winds blew all night long. The winds blew their dark night song across the world at night. Down the valleys they come far away and they blow far away down the valleys where no winds stay for long. And that is the sadness of their wind-blown song. Not for long, never for long. O best loved Bunny in all the world.

A DREAM

Bunnies and Bunnies and Rabbits ago
    In the Light Green Land of Me,
I was a Bunny and so were you
    And we lived in a hollow tree.
You were gray and I was white
    In that Light Green Land of Me,
And we slept all day and ran all night
    And lived in a hollow tree.

Copyright 1950 by Margaret Wise Brown and Elizabeth Randolph, under the title "The Light Green Land of Me."

NOTHING BUT BUNNIES

There was a World in which there were nothing but Bunnies. Everyone was a Bunny. The mothers and fathers were Bunnies, so of course the children were Bunnies. And the aunts and uncles were Bunnies, and the cousins were Bunnies, and of course all the brothers and sisters were Bunnies, and the babies were Bunnies, too. Everyone was a Bunny. And all day long, they went about their little Bunny busyness as usual. The World of Bunnies was made of green grass and sunshine and dandelions and the wild yellow carrots which, of course, grew under the ground.

In this World of Bunnies day was night and night was day, for night was the time for the Bunnies to run about in the darkness and the moonlight.

Houses were holes and roads were tunnels through the tall green grass. And feet were the fastest things to get around on. In this World everyone was a Bunny.

It would have seemed very funny not to be a Bunny.

HERE COMES A BABY

THE BUNNIES were expecting a baby.

"When will it be here?" asked the three little Bunnies.

"When it comes," said the Mother Bunny.

The three little Bunnies ran to the window to see if the baby was coming.

But they couldn't see it. Not there. Though one Bunny said he could see it on a cloud in the air.

Whose baby Bunny will it be?

"Here comes a baby," cried the fat little Bunny. "He's still far away but he looks rather funny. A little old baby as blind as a mole. Do you think there's room for another in our hole?"

"No room, no room," squealed the three little Bunnies.

"No," said the fat Bunny. "Not where I live. I don't want a baby and I'll pull its whiskers when it gets here."

"I'll sit on it if it sits in my chair," said the littlest Bunny, who really had a little chair.

"It could live in the garden," said the middle-sized Bunny. "It doesn't look very big."

The baby was always coming nearer. And, of course, they couldn't see it, but they pretended they could. And it came nearer and nearer.

"I'll sew it some clothes," said the Mother Bunny. "The clothes won't be very big."

"I'll make it a bed," said the Father Bunny. "The bed won't be very big."

"I'll pick it some flowers," said the fat little Bunny. "Little tiny flowers because its nose won't be very big."

"I'll build it a hat," said the middle-sized Bunny. "The hat doesn't have to be big."

The littlest Bunny didn't say a thing.

As they thought about it, the baby grew larger and the time for it to come was almost here.

"Here comes a baby," cried the little fat Bunny. "It can't sleep in my bed. There isn't room here for anyone but me."

"It can't have my blocks," said the middle-sized Bunny. "It can't play in my cabbage garden."

"It's very little," said the littlest Bunny. "We could find it a little acorn to play with."

"Here it comes, here it comes," cried the Father Bunny.

"Here it is," said the Mother Bunny. "It has hair and toes and eyes and nose and eyelashes."

"It's mine, it's mine," squealed the three little Bunnies.

"It can sleep in my bed," said the little fat Bunny.

"It can sit in my chair," said the littlest Bunny.

"But it can't be me," squealed the middle-sized Bunny. "But I'll give it the tiny flowers."

"It's mine, it's mine," cried the Mother Bunny.

"It's thine and mine," said the Father Bunny.

"It's ours," cried the whole Bunny family.

RABBIT
HOUSES

Once there was a little Rabbit.
Nobody brought him up.
He brought himself up
And he lived in a house
All by himself in the grass.

When he was bigger
He lived in a bigger house
In a wild tangled bog.
When he was bigger
He lived in a bigger house

At first his house was a little house
Just big enough for himself
As he grew.
When he was bigger
He lived in a bigger house
In a log.

Deep in a hollow tree.
When he was bigger
He lived in a bigger house
Down under the ground
Where no eye can see.

THE SNOWSHOE RABBIT

The Snowshoe Rabbit, white as white,
Runs over the snow in the bright moonlight
Invisible on the snow white hill
As the snow falls down until
The Snowshoe Rabbit runs around
Brown as the leaves
    on the old brown ground
And no one can see him
    running around
Brown as the leaves
    all over the ground.

A BIG WHITE
POWDERY WALK

By the dark gray river in the soft white snow
I caught a little Rabbit and let him go
Bounding deep in the deep soft snow.

THE FIRST SNOWDROP

Long before the robin dares
To flick his shadow across the ground,
When the roots are still asleep
And the cold winds creep
Over the cold still ground,
Suddenly among the leaves
Frail as air, yet
Bolder than a polar bear,
You will find
The first snowdrop,
Long before spring,
Long before anything
White and green
Blooming there.

RABBIT DREAM

Dream of a world as white as snow
Where little Rabbit footprints go
Hopping through the powdery snow,
powdery snow, powdery snow, whoa!

7 LITTLE HOPTOADS

SEVEN very little hoptoads went out for a hop all on a summer's day.

The first little hoptoad saw a big warm gray shadow. The second little hoptoad saw a big white animal with whiskers. The third little hoptoad saw two red shiny eyes and a short tail. The fourth little hoptoad saw two long soft ears. The fifth little hoptoad saw a little pink nose twitching. The sixth little hoptoad saw little white teeth nibbling a lettuce leaf. The seventh little hoptoad saw a bunny.

Then the seven little hoptoads hopped home to their home, all on a summer's day. They lived in a stump.

FIRE!
FIRE!
FIRE!

"Fire! Fire! Fire!" shouted Silly Bunny.
"Fire! Fire! Fire!"
The leaves in the woods
  were all blazing red.
Silly Bunny thought they were on fire.

"Boo!" said the red squirrel.
"Nuts, nuts, nuts, Silly Bunny!
The woods are not on fire. This is the
Fall of the year. Nuts fall down in the
Fall of the year. Leaves turn red in
the Fall of the year. Nuts, nuts, nuts."

Silly Bunny went down the road till he
  came to the garden.
In the garden the flowers were
  blazing red.

"Fire! Fire! Fire!" shouted Silly Bunny.
"Fire! Fire! Fire! The garden is on fire!
All the flowers are blazing red."

"Buzz, buzz, buzz,"
said the bee.
"The garden is not on fire.
Buzz, buzz, buzz.
Red flowers bloom in the Fall
of the year. Blazing red flowers
bloom and bloom. Buzz, buzz, buzz."

So Silly Bunny hopped up to the garden wall.
The sun was going down.
"Fire! Fire! Fire!" shouted Silly Bunny.
"The sun is on fire!"

"Who, who, who," said a sleepy old owl.
"Who woke me up?"
"Fire! Fire! Fire!" shouted Silly Bunny.
"The sun is on fire! The sun is blazing red."
"Who, who, who," said the sleepy old owl.
"You woke me up.
The sun is not on fire.
The sun is going down.
The sun is blazing red
when the sun goes down.
Go to sleep, Silly Bunny."

So Silly Bunny, who was sleepy,
went to sleep.
But the crickets woke him up.

All at once a big red ball of fire
    blazed in his face.
It was the moon.
"Fire! Fire! Fire!" called Silly Bunny.
"The moon is on fire!"

"Full moon, full moon,"
    chirped the crickets.
"Full moon, full moon,
The moon is full
In the Fall of the year,
In the Fall of the year.
The moon is full,
The moon is full
In the Fall of the year,
In the Fall of the year.
The moon is full
And the moon is red."

"Oh, dear," said Silly Bunny.
"I wish there was a fire.
I am getting cold."
And just then he saw a fire burning
    in the woods. Some children were
    cooking marshmallows.
And he went and sat by it.
"Fire! Fire! Fire!" shouted Silly Bunny.
"Yes," said the children.
"Come and warm yourself at our fire."

CROCUSES

Crocuses like Easter Eggs came bursting from the ground.
The snow was melting quietly, one Rabbit hopped around.
And the green grass was still asleep in the ground.

WHICH IS THE EASTER BUNNY?

The Easter Bunny is a funny Bunny
Whom no one sees, and that seems funny.
Which Bunny is the Easter Bunny?

A BUNNY'S

 **A** is for Apples, juicy and new.

 **B** is for Buttercups, easy to chew.

 **C** is for Carrots that crack when you eat.

 **D** is for Dandelions, yellow and sweet.

 **E** is for Eggs that don't make a sound.

 **F** is for Fruit when it drops to the ground.

 **G** is for Grasses beginning to grow.

 **H** is for Hay to eat in the snow.

 **I** is for Itch if you eat the wrong thing.

 **J** is for Juice of the small leaves in Spring.

 **K** is for Kale that is pretty with flowers.

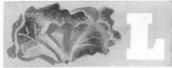 **L** is for Lettuce to nibble for hours.

 **M** is for Mushrooms all bouncy inside.

HUNGRY ABC

N is for Nuts that squirrels like to hide.

O is for Over the distant hill.

P is for Pansies the frost didn't kill.

Q is for Quinces that smell like a dream.

R is for Radishes, red as they seem.

S is for Sourgrass that tastes very good.

T is for Tansy that grows in the wood.

U is for Under the wild green grass.

V is for Violets and wild sassafras.

W is for Watercress in a swift running brook.

X is for What you can find if you look.

Y is for Yams that they eat in the South.

Z is for Zebras, and so close your mouth.

THE SLEEP RABBIT

There was a Rabbit who ran softly about the forest at sundown on his four fur feet, telling all the animals to go to sleep. You could hear him coming—

Hippety hop
Hippety hop
Hippety hop
Stop.
A little skunk had not yet gone to bed.

"What, little skunk," said the Rabbit softly, "are you still shuffling about? Time for all little skunks to be in their dry leafy beds.

"Good night, little skunk. Stop stinking and go to sleep."

Then—

Lippety lop

Lippety lop

Lippety lop

Stop.

Off went the Rabbit on his four fur feet, telling all the animals to go to sleep.

Until—

He came to a deep green tree.

And the Rabbit hollered high into the treetops of that deep green tree.

"Whoops—! You little red squirrels, stop all your frisking. Pop into your holes. Go to sleep!"

Silence—

Not a sound.

No branch snapped.

No nut cracked.

No leaf stirred.

"Asleep," whispered the Rabbit, and he went on his way through the great green forest over the soft green grass. You could hardly hear him on his soft fur feet.

Hippety hop

Hippety hop

Hippety hop

Hippety hop

Hippety hop

Stop.

A pig was watching the sunset.

"Grunt no more," said the Rabbit. "Little Pig, go to sleep."

And off went the Rabbit on his four fur feet. You could hardly hear him—Jiggety jig
       Jiggety jig
          Jiggety jig
            Stop.

He could hear a rumpus in a cave in the rocks.

Three little bears were tearing their hairs and growling and prowling about.

"Hush, little bears.
    Crawl into your lairs.
       Go to sleep."
B z z z z z z z z z z z z z z z z z z
   B z z z z z z z z z z z z z z z z z z
      B z z z z z z z z z z
The bees in the honey were making a funny B z z z z z z z z

"Hush, little bees. The sun goes down and the flowers grow cold and young bumble bees are not very old. The darkness arrives. Fly into your hives. Go to sleep, sleepy bees."

Silence.
    Not a sound.
        No branch snapped.
            No wave lapped.
                No leaf stirred.
    Then off went the Rabbit through
the soft dark night of the great green
forest, over the soft green grass. You
could hardly hear him.
        Hippety hop
            Hippety hop
                Hippety hop
                    Thud!
    The Rabbit bumped into another
Rabbit who was running softly about
the forest at sundown on his four fur
feet, telling all the animals to go to
sleep.
    Go to sleep, Rabbit
    Go to sleep, Rabbit
        Go to sleep
        Go to sleep
            to sleep
                to sleep
                    sleep
                    sleep
                    sleep
                    sleep.